Flora
the Fancy Dress Fairy

Daisy Meadows

ORCHARD

www.rainbowmagicbooks.co.uk

The Fairyland Palace

McKersey Castle

Jack Frost's
Ice
Castle

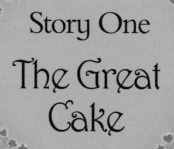

Story One

The Great Cake

The Great Cake

"What a beautiful place!"
Rachel Walker cried when
she saw McKersey Castle. Her
grown-up cousin Lindsay was
having a party there to celebrate
her wedding anniversary and
Rachel was invited, along with
her best friend, Kirsty Tate.

"It's just like a fairytale castle," Rachel said.

Kirsty grinned. She and Rachel knew all about fairies because they had met and helped the fairies many times!

Inside the castle, Lindsay showed them to their bedroom.

Rachel and Kirsty gasped with delight when they saw the huge room.

Lindsay pointed to a small door set opposite the beds. "That door leads up to the battlements," she said. "Be careful if you go up there!"

As Lindsay hurried off, Rachel opened the little door and found a staircase winding upwards.

Suddenly a chilly gust of wind blew right down into the room.

"Look, there's ice all over the stairs!" Kirsty gasped.

The girls were curious, so they climbed the steps, holding on to the handrail. The higher they got, the colder they felt.

"My Icicle Party will be the best fun ever!" snapped an icy

voice ahead of them.

The two girls crept to the top of the steps and peeped around a turret. They saw Jack Frost standing there!

"I'll be the one having a party tomorrow, not those pesky humans!" he said to the goblin servant beside him.

"We can't let Jack Frost spoil our party," said Kirsty. "Let's go to Fairyland and get help!"

The girls opened their special lockets and sprinkled fairy dust over their heads. The magical dust turned them into fairies and whisked them away.

As soon as Rachel and Kirsty landed in Fairyland, a fairy in a fabulous mermaid costume flew up to them.

"Oh, I'm so glad to see you!" she cried. "I'm Flora the Fancy Dress Fairy."

The girls said, "Hello!"

"Is something wrong?" Kirsty asked.

"Some goblins have stolen my magical items," Flora said. "I need them to make sure fancy dress parties go well. The magical figurine, a little golden model of a princess, makes food taste wonderful. The Red Riding Hood cape helps costumes look good and the third item is a mask with rainbow feathers that makes sure everyone has a fun time."

Rachel and Kirsty looked at each other in alarm.

"Flora, we know where your items might be!" said Kirsty. "I bet Jack Frost's goblins have taken them for his Icicle Party!"

"Then I'll magic you back to McKersey Castle, and we can all search for them," said Flora.

The girls were swept up in a cloud of fairy dust. A moment later, they found themselves standing on top of the castle.

Kirsty looked over the stone battlements at a van that was parked below.

"Look, goblins!" she said.

The cake shop van had its back doors open. As the girls and Flora watched, they saw three goblins climbing out. The goblins had a big cardboard box and they tore it open. Inside was a big white cake.

On top was a little figurine.

"They're stealing Lindsay's cake!" Rachel wailed.

"And my magic figurine!" said Flora. "Without it, all the food at the party will be spoiled!"

Flora whizzed down to talk to the cheeky goblins.

"Go away, pesky fairies!"
said one of the goblins. "We're
taking this cake for Jack Frost's
Icicle Party."

He broke off chunks of cake
and threw them at Flora and
the girls.

"He's ruining it!" Kirsty
gasped.

Then the other two goblins
began eating the cake with
their hands.

"Yum!" they said.

"Stop that!" the first goblin shouted. "Jack Frost's waiting for us."

"We should put the cake in the van," said another goblin.

The girls and Flora saw a different van parked nearby. It had 'Jack Frost's Frosted Delights' written on the side. The goblins ran over to it and began struggling to put what was left of the cake inside.

Flora, Rachel and Kirsty wondered how they could stop the goblins getting away.

Suddenly Rachel had
an idea. "If we lift up the
drawbridge, they won't be able
to leave the castle!"

"Brilliant!" said Kirsty.

The goblins had climbed
into their van and were driving
it away. But Flora waved her
wand and pointed it at the
drawbridge.

Magical sparks flew around the chains and the drawbridge lifted up.

The goblins were trapped inside the castle!

"Thanks, Flora!" said Rachel. "Let's get the cake!"

Quickly, Flora turned Rachel and Kirsty back to human size.

But before they could get to
the van and rescue the cake, the
goblins opened the back door.

"All right, have your stupid
cake!" one sneered.

They pushed the cake out –
SPLAT!

"Oh no!" cried Rachel.

The cake was ruined. But Flora's figurine was still in one piece.

"Those silly goblins forgot about the Icicle Party and just wanted to upset us," said Kirsty.

"Don't worry," whispered Flora. "Just wait until I get my magic figurine back."

Flora lowered the drawbridge. The goblins zoomed out of the castle in their van, blowing raspberries at the girls.

As soon as the van was gone,

Flora flew over to her figurine.

"Now, close your eyes and make a wish," she said.

The girls held hands and wished for the most beautiful cake ever made. When they opened their eyes again, it was standing in front of them!

Story Two

Colourful Costumes

Colourful
Costumes

The day of the anniversary
party had arrived.

"I'll show you the costumes,"
Lindsay said to Rachel and
Kirsty. "You can have first pick!"

Kirsty and Rachel followed Lindsay down a staircase and along a corridor to a sturdy wooden door.

"Enjoy choosing your outfits," she said. "I have to go and prepare for the party!"

"This will be fun," said Kirsty. She pushed open the door.

But the girls were shocked when they saw what was inside!

Two goblins were pulling costumes off racks and throwing them around the room.

"Stop that!" cried Rachel.

The room was a total mess. One rack had been knocked over, and the costumes were lying in a heap. The goblins saw the girls and grabbed piles of clothes. Then they climbed onto the window ledge.

"They're going to jump!" Kirsty shouted.

The goblins leapt out of the window and held onto a heavy rope which had been tied to a wardrobe.

The girls rushed to see where they had gone.

"Look!" Kirsty cried. She pointed at a boat in the moat.

In it were three goblins, ready to row it away.

"They've got Flora's magic cape!" Rachel gasped. She had spotted a piece of bright red material in the boat.

"Let's get onto the drawbridge and grab the cape as the goblins row past," Kirsty said.

The girls dashed down the stairs, and passed a suit of armour with an open visor. They could see a strange, sparkly glow inside. It was Flora!

"Hello, girls!" said the fairy as she flew out of the helmet.

"Where are you going?"

Rachel quickly told Flora what had happened and the three friends hurried to the drawbridge.

"We're going to lean over and grab the cape," Kirsty said.

"Good plan!" Flora replied.

Rachel and Kirsty lay down on the drawbridge. The boat with the goblins was close. Rachel reached out to snatch the sparkling red cape, but one of the goblins spotted them!

"They're trying to steal our

costumes!" a big goblin yelled.
"Stop rowing around in a
circle! Let's go to the bank!"

Kirsty, Rachel and Flora
watched in dismay as the
goblins rowed away.

"I nearly got the cape, too,"
Rachel said.

The girls ran across the
drawbridge. They were hoping
to catch the goblins on the
other side.

The goblins reached the bank
and threw the costumes out of
the boat.

"There are too many to carry!" one goblin shouted.

"Put on some of the clothes!" another goblin said.

Flora and the girls watched
in surprise as the goblins
dressed themselves up. They
looked ridiculous!

The costumes were far too big for the goblins. They had been designed for humans! One goblin put on a tiger outfit and a clown's nose. Another was wearing a pink wig with a golden crown on top. He also had Flora's magic cape tied around his neck. But the hood kept falling forwards over his face! All of them were wearing odd shoes and kept tripping up.

Flora, Rachel and Kirsty couldn't help laughing as they crossed the drawbridge and reached the bank.

"Give us those costumes!" Flora called.

"No!" came the reply. "Jack Frost's holding *his* party here tonight, so you won't need them for *your* party!"

Another goblin cackled in glee, then threw a dress over Rachel, Kirsty and Flora.

"Help!" Rachel cried, trying to struggle free.

The girls quickly untangled themselves from the dress. But by then the goblins had already run off.

They had left lots of costumes behind them on the ground.

"We can't leave them but there are too many to carry," said Rachel. She pointed at the scattered clothes.

Kirsty looked closely at a pretty jacket.

"The stitching on this is

coming loose!" she cried.

"The costumes are falling apart because my magic cape is missing," Flora explained. "If we get it back, I can fix them!"

"Can you shrink the clothes to pocket size?" Kirsty asked.

With a wave of her wand, Flora made the clothes tiny.

The girls could slip them into their pockets. Then they all rushed after the goblins. They ran towards a steep slope where some goats were grazing.

"Perhaps we can ask the goats to help us," Rachel suggested.

"Great idea!" Flora said.
"Animals like fairies."

Flora whispered to the goats.
They looked up and then
trotted over to the goblins. They
were blocking their path!

The goblins stared nervously at the hairy creatures. They shook with fear.

"They're very big," said one goblin.

"Do you think they eat goblins?" asked another.

One of the goblins was wearing a hat with a felt flower. A curious goat came over to sniff it.

"Baaa!" said the goat, and tried to eat the flower.

The goblins were terrified! They threw down all the costumes they were carrying and backed away in fear.

"What the goats really want is the clothes!" Flora told the girls. "They like to eat cloth."

The goats started sniffing the
goblins all over. The goblins
pulled off their clothes and held
them out. They wailed in fear.

"Don't eat me!" begged the
goblin with the cape. "This cloak
is much tastier than I am."

The goat snorted. Yelling with fear, the goblin threw down the cape and ran away. His terrified friends followed.

Quickly, Flora shrank the clothes and the girls gathered them up. Then they ran back to the castle. Flora began to sort out the mess in the room where the costumes were kept.

As the fairy flicked her wand, Rachel and Kirsty watched the clothes grow back to normal size and tidy themselves up.

"I must take my magic cape back to Fairyland," said Flora with a smile. "Meanwhile, you two need to get dressed for the party. Somewhere in this room my magic has sorted out perfect costumes for you!"

Rachel and Kirsty grinned at each other.

"Let's see what we can find!" Kirsty said.

Story Three

The Perfect Party

The Perfect Party

"Look, Rachel!" cried Kirsty.
She had spotted tiny magical
sparkles shimmering around a
clothes rail.

Hanging on the rail were
two angel costumes. They were
absolutely perfect!

The girls got dressed and went down to the ballroom. The decorations were white and gold. Marble statues wearing masks had been placed around the walls. The cake stood on a table in the middle.

"It's beautiful!" Kirsty said.

"I don't think any of these masks are Flora's magic one," said Rachel. "We must find it before the goblins do. Otherwise the party will be ruined!"

"Look up there," Kirsty cried. She pointed at the figurine on the top of the cake. "It's Flora!"

The figurine winked. But they didn't have time to say hello. Some rather odd guests had arrived.

"Goblins!" Rachel gasped.

"We're here for Jack Frost's party!" snapped one of the smartly dressed guests. He was holding up an invitation. "It's taking place here, tonight."

The girls glanced nervously at the invitation. It clearly read 'McKersey Castle'.

"Tell him to check it again!"
Flora whispered to Kirsty.
She waved her wand at the
invitation.

The goblin re-read the fancy
invitation and his eyes almost
popped out of his head.

"It says the party is at Jack
Frost's Ice Castle!" he muttered.

Invitation

Party at the

Ice Castle

The goblins all turned and left, miserably. It was just in time. Lindsay's real guests were arriving for her party.

"Grrr!" A growling sound suddenly made the girls look round. They saw a woman dressed as a tiger spring forward. She began sharpening her claws on a pillar.

"She's taking the dressing-up a bit too seriously!" Rachel whispered to Kirsty.

"People's costumes are going wrong because my mask is

missing," said Flora sadly. "Your fairy lockets are protecting you, but not the other guests. That woman thinks she actually is a tiger!"

Suddenly Lindsay rushed in. She looked upset. She was still wearing ordinary clothes.

"I went to put my costume on but I can't find my mask!" Lindsay said.

"We have to find the magic mask quickly," whispered Rachel. "Let's go and search!"

The girls tiptoed away from the party and began looking around the castle.

The girls walked up and down the corridors, but they found nothing. Then Kirsty spotted something pink at the bottom of a staircase.

"Look, goblin footprints –

and a tiny feather!" she said.

"It's from my magic mask!" whispered Flora.

The footprints seemed to stop dead in front of a wall.

"Do you think there's a secret passage?" Rachel asked.

The girls peered at the wall until Kirsty spotted a hole.

Kirsty put her hand into the hole and felt a little switch.

When she pressed it, the wall swung back. The three friends stared into a dark passageway.

Rachel and Flora followed Kirsty down the narrow corridor. But they just found a dead end.

"This is no good," said Kirsty.

"Let me check this wall," Rachel replied. She felt the stones and found another hole with a switch inside it.

Rachel pressed the switch and the wall moved a few centimetres, as if it was a door.

The girls peered into a

cave-like room. They could see
a familiar figure sitting on a
throne. He had the magic mask
in his hand.

"Jack Frost!" Kirsty said.
"We're going to ruin this
pesky party!" Jack Frost said.
He laughed nastily.

Kirsty opened the door a bit wider, and saw lots of goblins listening to Jack Frost.

"I'll run in and grab the mask," Kirsty said, trying to feel brave. She crept into the room. Jack Frost was shouting and waving the mask about. Kirsty was able to snatch it easily!

"Stop that girl!" Jack Frost roared. But Rachel had pulled the door closed behind Kirsty. He was too late!

The girls and Flora ran away down the passage. A few moments later they were back at the party.

"I can see Lindsay and Robert," Kirsty said. She pointed to a couple who were wearing fantastic king and queen costumes.

"Lindsay!" Kirsty called. "We found your mask."

"How dare you talk to me in such a rude manner?" Lindsay snapped.

Rachel and Kirsty stared at each other in confusion. "It's OK," Flora whispered. "She thinks she's a real queen. Try giving her my magic mask.

It will help."

"Your Majesty," said Rachel.
"We have brought you this
tribute!" She held out the mask.

Lindsay took it, and held
it up to her face. She blinked,
then seemed to wake up, as
though she'd been in a dream.

Linday was back to normal and soon the party was in full swing. All three of Flora's magic items had been found, so everything was sure to go well.

"Look over there!" said Kirsty. She pointed to someone dressed as a pirate. He had a spiky beard. With him were other guests with green faces.

"What amazing face paint!" the woman in the tiger costume said to them.

"Even Jack Frost and his goblins are joining in the fancy

dress party!" Kirsty laughed.

"Thank you so much for
all your help, girls," Flora said.
"I'm going to stay for the party
to make sure it goes perfectly."
And it did!

**If you enjoyed this story,
you may want to read**

Kylie the Carnival Fairy
Early Reader

Here's how the story begins...

It was the holidays and Rachel Walker was visiting her best friend Kirsty Tate. Today it was the grand opening of the

Sunnydays Carnival.

"This is so exciting!" said Kirsty. "Look at all the rides!"

"There's the Carnival Master," said Rachel. She pointed to a jolly-looking man in a top hat. He marched up to the gates and threw them open.

"Welcome!" he boomed. "Let the carnival magic begin!"

He pointed at the big wheel with his hat. Slowly the wheel began to turn. The other rides started moving, too.

"It's magic!" gasped a boy.

Rachel and Kirsty smiled.
They knew all about magic!
The two girls were special
friends of the fairies. But
spiteful Jack Frost and his
goblin servants liked to cause
trouble in Fairyland, so Kirsty
and Rachel helped the fairies

to sort things out.

A loud drum beat echoed through the air.

"Look at the parade!" Kirsty cried as a band marched by.

A man in a blue and gold peaked cap was leading the parade. He was carrying a rainbow-coloured baton...

Read
Kylie the Carnival Fairy
Early Reader
to find out
what happens next!

Meet the first
Rainbow Magic fairies

Ruby
the Red Fairy
Daisy Meadows

Amber
the Orange Fairy
Daisy Meadows

Saffron
the Yellow Fairy
Daisy Meadows

Fern
the Green Fairy
Daisy Meadows

Sky
the Blue Fairy
Daisy Meadows

Izzy
the Indigo Fairy
Daisy Meadows

Heather
the Violet Fairy
Daisy Meadows

Can you find one with your name?
There's a fairy book for everyone at
www.rainbowmagicbooks.co.uk

Let the magic begin!

RAINBOW magic™

Become a

Rainbow Magic

fairy friend and be the first to
see sneak peeks of new books.

There are lots of special offers and exclusive
competitions to win sparkly
Rainbow Magic prizes.

Sign up today at
www.rainbowmagicbooks.co.uk